DEAD AT SILVER LAKE

SALTED BY FIRE

TOM SCHNEIDER

D1523299

TOM SCHNEIDER

DAY BESTSELLING AUTHOR

DEAD

AT SILVER LAKE

SALTED BY FIRE

Dead at Silver Lake: Salted by Fire

ISBN: 9798364199973

Copyright © 2022 by Tom Schneider

For every one will be salted with fire.

MARK 9:49

1

October, 1933

His father banged on the bedroom door.

"You gonna get up, boy? Thought you're going fishing today?"

"I'm coming," Teddy yelled.

"Eggs are ready."

Teddy sat at the kitchen table and his father put a plate of fried eggs in front of him.

"I gotta run. I'll see you tonight," he said and he kissed Teddy on the head.

"Ok, Pops. We're gonna catch some snappers today, sell 'em to the Webers."

"Good, catch us some fish for dinner, while you're

at it, or better yet, trade those turtles for some dinner plates," he said, walking out the door.

Teddy ate his breakfast and thought about how he wished he could take his father out to dinner at the Silver Lake Inn where they could have lobsters, instead of fish from the lake. He ate his eggs and washed the plate in the sink.

———————

LINENS BLEW ON THE CLOTHESLINE. Hildegard walked out the back door of her house and down the porch steps to scatter food for the chickens.

Teddy stopped walking and leaned on the white rail fence at the end of the driveway. He could smell the sweetness of her hair drifting through the air.

"Good morning, Hildie!"

She looked up and half-waved.

The Webers owned The Silver Lake Inn. Most people just called it, "The Inn". Hildegard was the Weber's daughter and Teddy was smitten with her since he first saw her five years earlier at school when he was only twelve.

He walked down the road, behind The Barn, to Silver Lake. It was one of six lakes in Clementon that on warmer days served as popular swimming destinations for residents and out-of-towners from Philadelphia. Silver Lake boasted paddle-boats, bathhouses, and a thirty-foot slide into the water. This time of year there were only kids fishing or looking to earn a few bucks catching turtles for the Silver Lake Inn's snapper soup. He imagined the patrons sitting at tables with fine linens, sipping soup from their bowls. He pictured himself there, savoring the flavor.

Two men on the shore had lines in the water and there was one in a boat in the middle of the lake. He followed the path up the hill to Clementon Road. When he got to Reiner's Bakery, he glanced nonchalantly at it from across the street. He watched Dennis walk beside the building to the back. Dennis looked back and nodded before going behind the building.

Teddy adjusted his cap and stared into the shop window. He could taste the sugar from the doughnuts crackling on his tongue just thinking about them. Mr. Reiner was behind the counter and glanced through the window at him. Teddy looked away and started walking.

Around back, Dennis picked up an empty bottle from the steps. He backed up and smashed it into the backdoor. The bottle shattered. Teddy saw Mr. Reiner disappear from the storefront into the back. Teddy ran across the street into the bakery.

The clock chimed, and the cuckoo popped out and screamed. Teddy swiped a handful of doughnuts. He shoved them into his pocket, grabbed a few more, and ran out of the shop down the street.

Mr Reiner ran out the front door and yelled after him, and Teddy ducked into the woods. He met up with Dennis at the big rock and they sat, catching their breath before digging into their score.

"Dennis, you think if I had money, Hildie would go out with me?"

"Mmmm. Hildie. Now there's a tomato with some nice getaway-sticks."

"Knock it off. Don't talk about her that way," Teddy replied.

"What? Saying she has nice legs? Don't get goofy on me now. Why are you still dreaming of her? Just ask her out already."

"I can't take her anywhere. She's used to fancy restaurants and all that. She left the country before. But saying I could afford to take her out, you think she'd say yes?"

"Sure, why not?" Dennis said. "Her daddy ain't any better than moonshiners. He's selling their stuff. Selling the same stuff your pop is selling. He's buying your pop's hooch, for Christ's sake!" Dennis shoved his last bit of doughnut in his mouth. "He's just fancier about it, is all. You should ask her out, now."

Teddy was 17, he knew it was time he got serious. He was too old to be stealing doughnuts. It was time to build a future for himself. He couldn't make it as a moonshiner like his old man. Between the cops and the rackets, there wasn't any room for him to make a buck. They would squeeze little guys like his father out soon enough, if it didn't become legal again, which is what the rumor going around was. If he was going to ask her out, he would have to get proper work first.

Most of the jobs in town were at The Inn and Clementon Lake Park. There were others, but those were the biggest in town. Clementon was a lakeside resort town. There was a busy theater and several stages for top act performers and a lot of big names stopped on their tours. For some, it was a stop on the way to Atlantic City and for others; it was their final destination.

Silver Lake with 30' slide and bathhouse

2

Timber Lake was bigger than Silver Lake, and Teddy thought it was better fishing. Woods surrounded it and a single mansion that belonged to Al Capone faced the water. The yard started with a beach area, then grass that led to a large white fountain and the stone staircase to the back porch.

Teddy and Dennis sat with their bucket of turtles in their borrowed canoe, floating in the middle of the lake. Teddy ran his hand through the water.

"Hey, Dennis, do they need any help at the store? I need to get a job. Pop won't make much from the still once liquor is legal."

"No, not at the store, but Monk asked if I wanted to be a busboy. They're looking for one at the Silver Lake Inn."

"Really? Do they make good money?"

"It all depends on tips, but Monk says they do."

"They're all fancy in there, though I don't have nice enough clothes for the dining room," Teddy said.

"You don't need them. They do the laundry there and give busboys and even the cooks clothes to wear. I would take the job myself, but I kind of like it at the store and they pay well enough."

Sitting in the front, Teddy pulled his rod back and cast it when Dennis screamed behind him. The canoe rocked and nearly tipped. He turned around and saw Dennis holding his head and blood coming from between his fingers.

"oh, shit. Sorry."

"Get it out!" Dennis yelled.

Teddy stepped over top of the seat and pulled the hook from his scalp.

"Watch what you're doing," Dennis said as he took off his shirt and tied it around his head as a bandage.

They heard yelling from across the lake. A woman had come out of the mansion Al Capone's mansion. She was in an open robe, hurrying toward the lake and yelling to a man behind her. The man was large and swinging something in his hand. They stopped paddling and watched.

Their voices became clearer. The woman yelled, "Stay away from me, Bottles."

"I paid for you. I own you."

"I'm not a whore, Bottles. I loved you and it cost me everything," she said, crying.

She got to the lake and began walking in it.

"You want to drown yourself, you stupid bitch? Here, I'll help you," he shouted and pointed a pistol at her and fired two shots. The woman fell over into the water.

"Now it cost you everything," he said.

"Come on, let's get out of here," Dennis said.

They steered the canoe around and paddled toward the shore.

"Hey. Get over here, you little saps." the man yelled.

They paddled faster. They were almost at the beach when...

"You hear me. Get over here, you little bastards."

Four more shots rang out. One hit the trees on the shoreline and another hit the water. Then somehow they tipped the canoe and both landed in the water.

They pulled the boat to the shore, ran into the woods, and dove into the leaves.

"Holy crap. I thought Capone was in jail?" Teddy said.

"He is."

They watched the man return to the mansion.

"Come on, we have to go back and get the turtles," Dennis said.

"Are you crazy?"

"Those snappers will get us good money. Monk's going to work this afternoon. He can take them for us and collect."

"I can go with him and ask about that job," Teddy said.

Bottles walked back into the house.

"He's not coming back out. We can get them, now. The canoe, too."

"We have to tell someone about what we saw," Teddy said.

"Tell who?" Dennis asked.

"The police."

"I don't know. He tried to shoot us. I don't want him after me. You can't trust the police around here, you know that. They're all out to make a buck," Dennis reminded Teddy.

Dennis ran toward the canoe, and Teddy followed.

Capone's house on Timber Lake, Clementon, NJ

3

The turtles swung in the bucket as Teddy and Monk walked to the restaurant. Monk wore his white chef's uniform. They turned onto Smith's Terrace and down to the where the path met the road and they followed it to the creek that runs to Silver Lake.

"Do you think he'll give me the job?"

Monk kept walking and didn't answer. Teddy was pretty sure he nodded.

As they neared Ohio Ave, Teddy saw Dewey walking toward where his family lived in a bunch of Gypsy Wagons. He knew Dewey for years. Dewey was on the large side and they used to call him, 'Dewey, Dewey, fat and chewy.' He hollered his name and Dewey stopped and faced him. Teddy waved and Dewey just stared for a moment and then started running toward his home.

"What's wrong with him?" Teddy asked. "Hey, I'll catch up in a minute," he said and ran after him. As he cleared the trees, a door on the wagon slam closed. He wasn't sure which one Dewey lived in, but figured it was that one. He ran down the street to catch up to Monk.

They walked up past the barn and to the back stairs of the kitchen. A man stepped out of the basement carrying a crate of liquor. Teddy watched as he walked across the lot and into The Barn, which was a converted chicken barn that now served as a banquet hall. The second floor had a bar with limited access. A larger bar sat downstairs in the dining room. Waiters and busboys carried food from the Restaurant's kitchen, across the parking lot, to the Barn's kitchen. Liquor could take a quicker route with the electronic pipeline that went underground and delivered bottles with a push of a button.

The Silver Lake Inn had undergone several upgrades during prohibition. Air Conditioning was the latest, installed in the summer of 1933, to everyone's delight. Teddy hoped to become a busboy to get in on the lucrative tip money, though he'd settle for a cook or dishwasher even. Any job there would give him a chance to get more acquainted with Hildegard.

The pig-farmer pulled up with his truck and Teddy watched a guy spin the fifty-gallon barrels full of slop for the pigs and move them in line all by himself. For some reason that gave him confidence they would have some kind of job for him.

Horns from cars pulling into the lot blew behind him. A finely dressed wedding party left their vehicles and entered The Barn. Everyone always was at The Inn. You wouldn't know there were hard times from looking at the customers. The times didn't affect the guests visiting town. From The Silver Lake Inn to the Clementon Lake Park, everyone had the gayest time.

Teddy and his family knew hard times. With his mother gone young and his father picking up odd jobs and moon-shining, they've struggled his whole life. He wanted to put trouble behind him, at least for a shift. Even to serve their food or clean their plates. At least it might give a window into something better.

He pictured himself as a guest at The Inn, sitting beside Hildegard. The waiter brought them champagne. He made a toast; they had a sip and Hildegard leaned in and kissed him on the cheek. It felt so close he could taste it.

Postcard stating, "the greatest outing and banquet resort in South Jersey, on the famous White Horse Pike, the boulevard from Philadelphia to the Atlantic."

4

The bell rang above the door when Nelson entered the coffee shop. He had a cup of coffee and a doughnut at a table near the window, and watched people walk by. He finished and walked down the street to his car.

The sun was in his eyes when he pulled up on the side of the road in front of Bottles Capone's office in Chicago. He squinted and pulled his hat down to block the rays and hide his face as he waited to see him exit the building.

A day earlier Nelson had gone home to surprise his wife and have lunch with her. He parked in front of their house, got out of the car, looked at the clear blue sky, and took a deep breath. He carried flowers to the door, smiling with thoughts of romancing his wife, Lilian.

As he got close to the house, he heard sounds from

inside. His heart dropped. He went in and followed the sound of his wife moaning, saying, "Bottles, Bottles,". The bedroom door was ajar, and he saw his wife in his own bed with Bottles Capone on top of her.

H slammed his fist down on the steering wheel. He wished he had killed him right then, but he backed up quietly and left without letting them know he was there. His own shame overwhelmed him and now his anger had taken its place, fully.

He suspected her of having an affair, but rationalized away his suspicions. His only focus was on raising a family with her. A year earlier she somehow lost a baby very early on. He tried to understand what happened, but she never wanted to discuss it. Now he knew his dreams of a family were gone, forever.

He reached, pulled the pistol from the glove-box, and studied it before looking up again to see the office door open and two men exit. Bottles was the third.

Nelson watched him as he stopped atop the steps and lit a cigar. The others waited at the bottom of the stairs. Nelson didn't care what happened after he finished what he was there for. Bottles had ruined his life and he was there to return the favor.

He climbed out of the car. The sun hit his eyes. It was a hot day. He felt the sweat from his arms sticking to his suit jacket as he walked up the street.

Nelson was in front of the building when bottles

walked down the stairs. The men walked around to the back of the car. One of them opened the passenger door for Bottles when Nelson yelled, "Bottles, you piece of shit!"

Nelson fired three shots. One went through the car window next to Bottles, another hit the man behind bottles in the head and he collapsed. Bottles and the other two drew their guns and returned fire. Capone and his Brunos emptied their guns before stopping.

5

It was dream come true–his first shift at the Silver Lake Inn. He followed the other busboys to the basement. Near the laundry was a rough cut room that looked like a cave, with walls carved out of rock by hand. They got changed and stored their clothes on the dirt floor along the edge of the walls.

Upstairs, the kitchen was a madhouse full of noise from the sound of pots being thrown down the line from the cooks' station to the pot washer. It seemed to be a sport. The pans skipped down the line and the pot washers had to jump to keep from getting bruised ankles. There was yelling everywhere and the worst language he'd ever heard. Giovanni from Sicily and Kris from Greece, the two head-waiters argued at the coffee machines. The cooks fought with the waiters and the dishwashers with the busboys.

Through the swinging doors to the dining room was another world. The orchestra played softly, people murmured, and the waiters that were exploding in the kitchen seconds before were serving patrons with grace. Silverware was placed quietly on linen-covered tables. Conversations muted, pleasantries filled the air.

He grabbed a tray from the dish rack and practiced balancing glasses with his back facing the kitchen door when someone in heels walked behind him. She circled around into the dining room. It was Hildie. He followed and saw that she was working in the coat-room. He walked to the dining room, clearing dirty plates and glasses as he fortified his nerves to talk to her.

On his third trip back from the kitchen, he walked into the lobby to the coat-check. When his eyes met hers, time slowed, and she froze in almost a nervous fear for a brief second.

After saying hello, it was like they were in on a secret. There was an instant trust and honesty between them. No longer an awkward space, they had to navigate. They were together.

Later in the evening he told her what happened at the lake.

"Teddy, you have to tell someone. You can't just watch a woman get murdered and go on about your day. You can't let a murderer get away with it."

"I don't know who to trust," he said.

"Well, you're going to have to decide and do some-thing, Teddy."

"I know. I know."

———

THE BAR WAS kidney-shaped with the bartenders in the middle. The Inn's parking lot and White Horse Pike were visible from the windows around the bar. Teddy entered the bar area with his tray and got in line behind another busboy and two waiters. He couldn't really believe he was working there as a busboy, and considered pinching himself when out of the corner of his eyes he saw the police chief they called Lutzie, sitting at the bar. He walked over to him.

"Excuse me, Chief Lutz?"

The chief turned around on his stool and stared at him.

"It doesn't look like you have my food. Did they run out?"

"No... I don't know."

"What do you want, then?"

"I saw something that you should know about."

"Oh, what's that?"

The entrance door over the chief's shoulder burst

open and Teddy froze as the large man he saw at the lake strode toward him.

"Bottles. Back in town again?" the chief asked as he brushed Teddy aside and embraced the man. Teddy stood in shock and then walked back to wait in line at the service bar. He looked back and saw the man he called "Bottles" with his arm around the chief's shoulders as they leaned against the bar.

After dropping off his drinks, he went and cleared a table forty-seven. At least he thought it was forty-seven. It was hard remembering all the table numbers. He stared into the foyer, hoping to glimpse Hildegarde.

He put the dishes and silver on the rack by the dishwasher. One of them was cleaning up a broken dinner plate. Fritz, the manager, was yelling at him, telling him how much each dish cost.

"Dummkopf," he yelled. "Maybe you'll start paying me for every dish you break. Then you won't break so many. If I find one more fork in the slop bucket, there will be hell to pay."

Teddy went back to the dining room with a new tablecloth. He replaced the linens and set the silver, glancing up strategically toward the cloakroom. She motioned for him to come see her.

He finished setting the table and walked through the foyer to fill her in.

"What happened? I saw you in the bar talking to

the Chief Lutz," she asked, pulling him into the cloak-room, where she pushed him back into the coats and out of sight.

The bell rang behind her and she went to the counter, took the gentleman's ticket, and got him his coat.

"Thanks, sweet cakes," he said.

"Have a great night, Mr. Gibbs," she said.

Hildegard turned and grabbed Teddy's arm.

"Tell me what happened," she said.

"He came into the bar and called for him as I was telling him,"

"What? Who did?" She asked.

"I have to go. Someone's going to look for me."

"Who came in?"

"Bottles," he replied.

"What?"

"I got to go. We'll talk later, when I get off."

———

LATER, Teddy walked back to the coat-check room to see Hildie.

"Hey, they let me off first, since I'm the new guy. I did alright with tips," he said.

"Great. I'll be here for a while. You can stay and talk," she said.

He moved behind the cutout wall to stay out of view. He told her what happened with Chief Lutz and Bottles, and it wasn't long before Teddy was thinking about other things, with his tips burning a hole in his pocket.

"Hey, Hildie. Can I take you to the movie sometime?"

"Sure. I could go tomorrow," she said.

"Deal."

Silver Lake Inn, Clemention, NJ

6

Teddy walked down the hill toward the lake, unsure what he was doing there but he wanted to know if he saw what he saw. He had to be certain before he told anyone else about it.

Meanwhile, he had an itch on his back, in a just out of reach spot, driving him crazy. He backed up against a tree and moved around frantically to scratch it.

Someone was coming up toward him from the lake. He stopped rubbing his back on the tree and squinted. It was a woman. She was wearing a long, open coat and stumbled as they got nearer. He was confused. She looked like the woman he saw get shot, as though she just crawled from the lake. Drenched with her feet covered in mud, she looked downward and didn't notice him at first.

When she looked up, she jumped backward and gasped.

"Oh. You scared me."

Teddy stood stunned, and they stared at each other before she spoke again.

"You know. You know what happened, don't you? You saw the whole thing," she said.

"What? Are you...?"

The woman shook her head. "I need a drink. I'll see you later, pal." And she continued walking up the hill past him.

Teddy stared at her until he heard the police siren behind him coming from the lake.

The chief's Plymouth Sedan squad car came to a stop over the dam at the end of the lake. When he looked back, the woman was gone. Ducking down low and he walked toward the lake to get a better view. On his knees, he watched as men fished out the body. It was the woman. The one he thought he just saw. The one he saw shot a couple days before.

He laid back on the ground and stared at the sky through the branches overhead, wondering what just happened? And who the woman was that spoke to him? What did she mean he saw the whole thing? Was it really her? Who was the woman being fished out? And why was the one that walked by him in the lake? And why did they look the same?

Clementon Theatre, Berlin Road

7

They walked together to the center of town. They got to the Clementon Theatre and past the movie poster for *The Invisible Man*, by H. G. Wells with the on-screen debut of Popeye the Sailor Man in *I Yam What I Yam*.

The theater was just five years old but featured vaudeville acts and photoplays, and boasted the largest theater organ in the area to accompany the silent pictures.

People out for the night crowded the sidewalk. Hildegard was beautiful. Not the freckled little girl he first met. She was a full grown woman, now. And tonight she dressed the part. He felt like the luckiest man alive, like he must be dreaming. He got everything he wanted; a new job, his dream girl. They stood in the back of the line and he stared at her profile and the world melted away around her. Then she snapped him back.

"You saw her ghost," Hildie said.

"What? I didn't say that."

"Well, what was she then?"

"She didn't look like a ghost."

"What do ghosts look like?" She asked.

"I don't know. You said she was a ghost, not me."

"So it wasn't her? It was a different woman?"

"It sure looked like her. She wasn't all shiny or see-through. I thought it was her. She looked like she walked out of the lake. Like it had just happened."

Hildie moved closer to him, and he looked down at her hand on his arm.

"I swear I could have reached out and grabbed her arm. I could see the lake water still on her."

"Was she pretty?"

"Yeah, good-looking woman, but she wasn't in her best shape. I can tell you that. She was stumbling like she was still drunk."

"Was there blood?"

"I didn't see any blood, I don't think."

"She told you, you know what happened. She wants you to tell the police what happened. You will be a hero."

"Or I'll be dead. Then my ghost will come and haunt you."

He grabbed her by the hips, pulled her close, and kissed her.

The line moved, and they entered the theater. Teddy was awestruck by the marble lobby and staircase to the balcony. He waited while she went to the powder room. She said they made the restroom of marble, too.

They took their seats with the ten-foot wide chandelier hanging over their heads. The lights went out, and the film rolled.

Hildie loved the picture, but had to remind Teddy to get his eyes on the screen when she caught him staring at her instead. After the show, they walked home, hand-in-hand, while the stars shined above. The temperature was pleasant, and the walk felt like he was gliding on clouds.

"Imagine being invisible, Teddy?" She asked. "Have you ever felt that way? Like people couldn't see you?"

"I guess I haven't thought about it like that," he said.

"I think about all the time," she said. "It's like some things only some people can really see. Others could walk right through something and never know it was there."

"I don't think I'd like that," Teddy said. "Not being seen, I mean. Seeing things wouldn't be so bad."

"I guess you're right," she said and squeezed tighter on his arm.

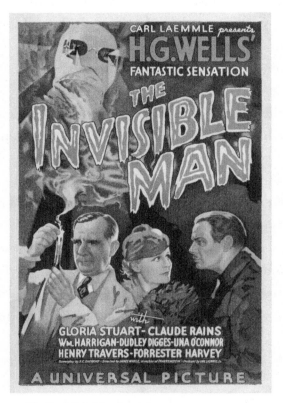

The Invisible Man (1933) poster

8

In the dining room of The Inn, the walls were lined with windows on two sides on what they called *The Porch*. The seating there was a little more private. In the corner was table sixty-five, where Bottles sat. His entourage filled three more tables in both directions. Teddy took the step up onto the porch when his eyes met Bottles. He felt a chill run through his body, and he froze still.

"Hey kid, come here," Bottles said.

"Yes, sir," he said as he navigated the tables and approached his side. "What can I get you?"

"You look familiar. I feel like I've seen you somewhere before."

"I was here the other night when you came in," Teddy said.

"No, it's not that. I felt it when I saw you then. It must have been somewhere before that."

"Oh, I didn't know you saw me then."

"I saw you through the glass door before I entered the bar. You were talking to my friend, the police chief."

"Was I?"

"Is there any snapper soup back there tonight?" Bottles asked.

"I'm not sure."

"Go find out and bring me some. Make it if you have to. You can go catch some turtles down at my lake and cook them up," he said and laughed.

"Yes, sir."

Teddy went to the kitchen and the chef prepared a bowl of soup and crackers. The itch on his back was bothering him again. He spotted a pair of salad tongs on the table and used it to reach the spot.

"You know who that is, right?," the chef asked. "Get him whatever he wants and don't piss him off whatever you do. Just keep your mouth shut. Only speak if spoken to. And even then, don't."

Teddy dropped the tongs, put the soup on his tray, grabbed a bottle of sherry, and went back into the dining room to deliver it.

He carefully placed the soup in front of Bottles and backed away when he was called again.

"Kid, come here. What's your name?"

"Teddy."

"Teddy, huh? Hey, I saw you talking to the coat-check girl earlier. You sweet on her?"

Teddy smiled.

"You are. Are you dating her?"

"I took her to the theatre."

"Downtown? What did you see?"

"The Invisible Man."

"Was it good?"

"Yes, sir."

"Did you get a little action? Haha. You don't have to answer that... You should take her to the drive-in theatre."

"The park-in?" Teddy corrected him.

"What's that?" Bottles asked.

"I think they call it a park-in."

"Whatever the hell they call it... Listen, kid. You take her to the drive-in and that way you won't even know what happens in the movie. You have privacy in the car. Know what I mean?"

"Oh, I don't have a car," Teddy said.

"You know what? I have plenty of cars. You can take mine. When are you off next?"

"I couldn't..."

"Don't fight me Teddy. You won't win. You're

going to take my damn car. I'm going to leave one here tonight for you."

———————

It was the end of the night and Teddy finished setting tables for the next day and walked to the bar with a stack of trays. The woman he saw murdered was sitting alone at the bar. The bartender wasn't there. She sat on a stool, hunched over the bar, with her legs crossed, and her hands clutching a glass.

He stacked the trays, walked over to her, and leaned on the bar beside her.

"Hello," he said.

She turned toward him and gave a half-smile.

"Hello, want to join me?" She asked.

He sat down beside her and stared at her while she looked ahead. He looked at her arm and placed his hand on her wrist. She turned her head and looked at him. He pulled his hand away.

"I'm sorry. I had to see if you were real."

"Is that some kind of line? I'm as real as you are."

"I'm sorry, you look like someone I saw... never mind."

"Are they still serving in the Barn tonight? It's getting a little quiet here."

"I'm not sure. Probably. There's usually someone down there after this place is closed."

She put her empty glass down and stood up. He couldn't help but stare at her breasts as she rose. As she turned slightly, her blouse opened enough for something to catch his eye and make him shutter. It couldn't be, but what he saw appeared to be a bullet wound.

He watched as she walked to the door. She pulled it open, looked back, and winked. Teddy raised his hand to wave. He really was confused. He was sure he saw her shot at the lake. It couldn't have been her. He was certain it was the same woman he saw when he went back to the lake.

He went to see the car that Bottles left. He considered leaving it there to avoid having to explain it to his father. It was only five blocks to his house down near Bottoms Lake, but he didn't want to be ungrateful and anger Bottles. He's seen him angry, and it wasn't pretty. He got in the car and closed the door. As he drove out of the parking lot, he thought it was nice being out of the cold. He went down Ohio Ave and past Hildie's back driveway. He was excited to take her to the park-in.

Ralph "Bottles" Capone.

9

Teddy sat up from his bed, looked around the room, and listened. It was quiet. He was surprised his father didn't call for him to get up like he usually did before he left. He expected to have to answer him about whose car he parked in front of the house, but everyone was asleep when Teddy got in and apparently gone before he awoke.

While he had the car, he decided to take a quick ride out to the lake. He was drawn back there, and like Hildie said, maybe he would see something he didn't before.

He drove out past the Clementon Lake Park as people were streaming in the main entrance, and he headed down Berlin Road toward the lake, past The Homestead Inn, and Reiner's Bakery. He hoped not to run into Bottles or have the car seen, so he parked in the woods after Old Mill Road.

He hiked through the woods toward the lake. As the water came into view, so did the flashing light from the top of the chief's car. Parked in the same place, over the dam as when he saw them fish out the body of the woman. It was like he was having déjà vu. He looked around him as if he expected to see the woman again, but he was alone. He sat on the ground and watched.

Two men walked to the other side of the dam after two more vehicles arrived at the scene. He watched until they came back up, carrying a body.

He stood and tried to get a better view. It wasn't déjà vu. It wasn't the woman. The body was a male. He could see the legs in pants stick out from the sheriff's arms. He sat back down and rubbed his eyes.

Another? It couldn't be from the same time. There was no one else on the lake that morning besides him and Dennis. It must be an unrelated incident. Maybe they had simply fallen over the Dam and died from hitting the rocks below. Or else his new 'friend' Bottles was disposing of more people in the lake.

He wished he hadn't told Hildie anything about the lake or Bottles. She was pressuring him to tell the police what he saw. It was the right thing to do, but he didn't want to be the next person fished out of the lake. Bottles was turning out to be an okay guy.

Unsure what to do, he was going to use his car to take Hilde to the park-in theatre, come Hell or high water.

Meanwhile, a car approached from the Capone house and the chief waved him on and tipped his hat. Teddy walked back up the hill toward his car. A flock of blackbirds sat in the trees overhead and squawked at him as he walked beneath.

He drove through town, up Aerial Road, where he turned into the woods and went back to his father's stills. He wanted to see him. He walked through the trees. There was a smashed jar on the roots of a tree. Farther, he saw more broken glass, copper tubing on the ground, and then split barrels. There was no one around.

It had been a couple years since his father had a still confiscated. But they usually take everything. *This was different. Maybe since everyone thought prohibition was ending, they weren't bothering to collect the stuff?*

He looked around, puzzled, and returned to the car.

———

LATER THAT NIGHT AT WORK, it was getting near closing when Teddy was in the coatroom making plans with Hildie when they heard the scream and breaking glass. Lights from squad cars out front, flashed through the glass doors and reflected on the mirror in the lobby. Hildie grabbed his wrist as she ran toward the dining room. Teddy followed her into a closet passage to the kitchen that entered beside the cellar stairs. They went down and wound through two rooms and past the laundry area before Hildie climbed into a crawlspace and he followed.

As they crawled through the dark, Teddy asked, "Hildie, what's going on?"

"It's a raid."

"But the police are always here?"

"Probies–prohibition agents. They're not the locals. They're harder to buy off."

They kept crawling until they reached a trapdoor above them. Light shined through the cracks between the boards. Hildie struggled to lift it and Teddy helped push it open, and knocked a chair over that was on it. He got out and closed the lid, realizing they were in the Barn. He followed her through a narrow hall where two men came down a chute from the second floor. They all climbed out a small side door into the yard behind the building.

"C'mon Teddy, let's go to the lake."

Together, they ran across the parking lot into the darkness toward Silver Lake. They got to the lake, sat on the bank, and laughed.

"Holy cow. I didn't know there was a tunnel. And a getaway chute in the barn?"

"I love that chute," Hildie said. I used to play on that when I was younger.

"What's going to happen?" Teddy asked.

"Oh, nothing. Someone didn't get their payment or something. My father is going to be pissed, that's for sure. And the Chief will hear about it. He's supposed to find out when they're coming."

"Well, then it's probably not a good time to talk to the chief for a while."

"Teddy, you need to talk to him. You saw a woman get shot, and the body fished out."

"There was another one."

"What?"

"I was there today, and I saw them pull another body from the dam."

"Oh, my God. What does that mean?" She asked.

"Hey do you want to go for a walk? There's a path through the woods here that goes right to my house."

"In the dark?" She asked.

"There's some moonlight," he said.

"Okay, that commotion will go on for a while yet. But then we have to get back."

He lead her through the path he traveled for years. He grew up playing everyday along that path following the creek. Jumping across it, swimming in it, destroying beaver dams and building some of his own. He held the branches back for her and carried her through the patch of skunk-cabbage. They followed a trail on the edge of the creek where it fed into Bottoms Lake and right into Teddy's yard. He walked her to the hammock, and they swung back and forth, staring at the moonlight reflecting on the lake.

Clementon Park, 1933

10

The wind blew through the Ford's open windows as Nelson drove east. He was enjoying the bright sky and fair weather through the hills of Pennsylvania when he saw an oncoming vehicle hit a dog running across the road. Nelson slammed on the brakes, skidded in the dirt on the side of the road, and got out. The car that hit the dog continued down the road and the dog laid in the street.

He let a couple of cars pass and crossed to check the dog. It was not breathing. Nelson picked up the dog and carried it into the grass. He set it down gently on the ground. The dog lifted its head, stood up, and wandered off toward the tree line. Nelson watched it reach the trees and then returned to his car.

He got back on the road and drove until sunset when he pulled into a roadside motel. Inside, he surveyed the room, walked to the bed, sat down, took his shoes off, and laid on top of the covers, out straight like a corpse.

He closed his eyes and thought back to their wedding day. He stood on the steps of the courthouse, gave Lilian a kiss, took her hand and they went down the steps as their neighbors stood in as witnesses and threw rice at them.

––––––

AFTER SLEEPING A FEW HOURS, Nelson sat up and put his feet on the floor. He put on his shoes and looked around the room. The nightstand drawer was open and he pulled out the Bible. He flipped it open and read a random line.

> *but if you do not forgive others their*
> *trespasses, neither will your Father*
> *forgive your trespasses.*

He dropped the Bible on the floor, stood, and walked out the door. In front of the room, he took in a breath and adjusted his hat. He looked at his 1932 Ford.

Music was playing from down the end of the

motel. It was coming from a radio inside the Pierce Silver Arrow idling in front of the office.

He walked past the other rooms to the car, opened the driver-side door, got in, and drove onto the highway. A man ran out of the office and into the road, yelling. Nelson turned up the radio and floored the gas.

11

Teddy was behind the bar washing glasses when Nelson walked in the door with his hat tipped down, hiding his face. As the bartender approached him, he pulled out a photograph from his jacket pocket and placed it on the bar. The bartender picked it up and stared at it before dropping it down again, shaking his head. Teddy took a stack of glasses and walked to where he could see the picture.

Nelson noticed him looking and pushed the photo across the bar, closer to him.

"Have you seen her? Take a good look."

Teddy recognized her as the woman he saw murdered, later emerge from the lake, and at the bar. He stared at her and finally pushed it back toward the man.

"No, sir."

"You stared at her long enough," Nelson said.

"Sorry, she looks like someone else, is all."

"Someone else? Who?"

"Just some woman that came in," Teddy said.

"Came in here? When?" he asked.

"Yesterday, but it couldn't have been her."

"No? Why couldn't it have been her?"

"I mean, the woman looked different. It was a different woman," Teddy said as he took his tray and walked toward the dining room.

He went to the kitchen and cleaned out the bread warmer, saving the leftover pieces for Emma to make croutons and breadcrumbs.

TEDDY LEFT out the back door and went down the parking lot past the barn to Bottles' car. He lit a cigarette and made a right out of the back lot to go pick up Hildie. She jumped up at the car window, giving him a scare, and he dropped his cigarette.

"Oh shit," he said, reaching down to get it before burning the seat. He took a drag, flicked it onto the road, got out and gave her a hug and a kiss. He walked her around to the passenger side and let her in. Then they drove up Aerial Road to where he could park with a view of Philadelphia.

He pulled out a flask from his pocket, held it up for

her to view, and smiled. She reached up and snatched it from his hand. They snuggled and traded sips for a while.

"Well, if you saw the girl from the picture, here, after you saw the body in the lake–then it couldn't be the same girl, right?"

"Except it was. I know it was."

"What if it was, Teddy?"

"What if it was?" He repeated. "Can't be, I don't know. Funny thing is there was a guy at the bar earlier tonight looking for her. He had a picture of her and I said I never saw her."

"Oh, my God. Why didn't you tell him?" Hildie asked.

"What am I going to say? I saw your girlfriend shot and killed, then fished out of the lake a few days later. But don't worry, she was at the bar drinking later, and stick around she may come back again?" he asked Hildie.

"I don't know. I couldn't even explain it. Explain it to him. And I was kind of hoping it wasn't her."

Teddy leaned against her, and Hildie gave him a hug.

"Teddy, you have to start being honest. With every-one. Even yourself," she said.

"Hildie, do ma a favor and scratch my back up near my shoulder? I have an itch and I can't really reach it."

He used his arm to reach it and show her the spot, and she scratched it for him.

TEDDY TOOK Hildegard back before she got in trouble and watched her go inside. He pulled into the lot after seeing the lights still on in the Barn.

He walked to the kitchen entrance after the main door was locked. He entered the empty banquet area and up the steps. The bartender looked his way when he entered the bar and walked out past him.

At the bar sat the man with the pictures earlier. Teddy approached the man as he sat with his hand clutching his whiskey glass, and took the stool next to him.

"You're still around?" Teddy asked.

"I was going to ask you that. Name's Nelson. Don't think I caught yours?"

"Teddy. Good to meet you. I saw the light on and... well, anyway, I may have something to tell you," Teddy said.

"You do, huh? You seemed to stare at the photo like you recognized her. What do you know?"

"Not much, but I saw her."

"Where?"

"The last time was here, actually."

"Here? When?"

"In the restaurant, at the bar. Yesterday."

"Of course, at the bar. Who was she with?"

"No one. She was sitting alone."

"Not with Bottles?" Nelson asked.

"You know Bottles?"

"He's on my list to see, too."

"No, she wasn't with him. Not this time," Teddys said.

Nelson downed his glass and refilled it with the bottle.

"How about you tell me the complete story? Go back to when you first saw her."

"May I see the picture again?" Teddy asked.

"Sure," he said, placing it on the bar in front of them.

"Teddy, meet Lilian. Though I suppose you've already met," Nelson said. "I'm not surprised. She gets around."

The First "Park-In" Theatre Crescent Boulevard, Pennsauken, NJ

12

The rush was over in the dining room. Things were winding down, except for Weber's table. It was a ten-top table filled with his friends just getting started for the night. Mr. Weber stood, raised his glass, and gave a toast.

"Best while you have it, use your breath. There is no drinking after death," he said to cheers of "Prost" and they all drained their glasses. Most of them were at the bar a few hours and would probably go back after they ate.

Teddy wandered back to the coatroom to see Hildie. He pulled her close to him and kissed her. Together, they fell back into the coats and onto the floor. Teddy reached up and pulled a long overcoat down over the top of them while he kissed her. They rolled around a bit before he moved his hand up her stomach to her breasts.

Hildegard pushed away his hand and stood up.

"You are crazy, Teddy. Someone could come around that corner any second. My father could come around, for goodness' sakes."

Teddy got up, and Hildegard hung the coats on hangers.

"Now you better go. If he catches you here he'll kill us both," she said.

"Okay, I'm going... Oh, but I saw that guy and told him the truth, like you said."

"You did? He talked to you?" she asked.

"Yeah, he talked to me," he said, giving her a strange look.

"What did he say?" she asked.

He's pretty mad, I think. He's looking for Bottles, too. But I don't think it's because he misses him."

"Oh my," Hildie said. "I don't know about this mystery woman, but Bottles Capone shouldn't be too hard to find."

"No, I suppose not. Especially since I told him how to get to his house at the lake," Teddy said.

"You told him you saw Bottles shoot her?" she asked.

"Yes. I told you I was honest about it, like you said."

"I know, I know. It's just, wow... What is he going to do?" she asked.

"I don't know," he said. "Honestly, he seems a little crazy. I wasn't sure I should tell him where Bottles' house was, but I thought about that after I told him what I saw, so I was stuck."

"Well, you certainly keep things interesting, Teddy."

Teddy pulled an empty hanger and used it to scratch his back.

"That's still bothering you?" she asked.

"Yeah, I don't know what it is, it's driving me crazy."

Pictured center-left bottom, Silver Lake Inn owner John Weber. Head-waiter and future owner, William F Schneider pictured top-right, under the banner, "Best while you have it use you're breath, there is no drinking after death."

13

Bottles' car pulled up in front of the mansion in Camden and the car with four of his men pulled behind. The car doors opened and the men all got out. Four men came out the front door and stood at the top of the porch. Bottles looked around at his men and waved them off. They all relaxed and drivers both sat in the cars. Bottles hiked his pants and adjusted his hat before walking up the stairs. He nodded and one of the men opened the door.

Bottles went down the hall, entered the room, took off his hat, and held it in his hands in front of him. He was much more demure than usual. Manoff Cinn sat in a cushioned chair in front of him. He was filing his nails and didn't look up.

"Hello, Mr. Cinn, I brought your package."

"Put it on the table," Manof instructed.

Bottles spotted a table across the room, walked to it, and placed an envelope from his jacket on the table.

"Ralphie, it seems you still haven't delivered what I really want. You recall what I asked for, don't you?"

"Yeah, about that, it's a little more complicated and could take a little time. It's not so easy..."

He appeared right in Bottles' face as fast as a cat. Bottles froze and felt a chill come over him. Manof put his hand on Bottles between his shoulder and his neck. Bottles felt a jab of pain and an increasing pressure, like a vise.

"I think you forget who you're talking to some-times, Ralphie. And the true nature of our relationship. If you cannot deliver for me, then I don't really need you here. You recall I have a great deal of leeway in our bargain. And things needn't be so pleasant for you."

The pain in his neck became unbearable. Bottles broke into a sweat and was visibly shaking. A fear he rarely experienced had grabbed a hold of his entire body until his knees buckled and hit the floor. He wanted to kill Manof, but he could not move.

"Yes, sir. I haven't forgotten anything. I will make it happen. You'll get him, I promise."

Manof removed his hand and Bottles let out a sigh of relief. He wiped his brow and stood, put on his hat, and hurried out of the room. He went through the hallway and out the front door. One of his men opened the car door for him and they drove out of town.

14

It was late when Teddy walked from the restaurant. He heard wood breaking behind the Barn and went down the parking lot to see what was happening.

There was a small door that entered the crawlspace under the building. Someone had kicked in the door and seemed to crawl around inside. He assumed to look for liquor. Teddy looked around at the empty parking lot and at the closed restaurant.

Inside, the man man fumbled in darkness and set his hand on the dirt floor when he heard a Timber Rattlesnake. He jumped up and hit his head on the rafter as more snakes joined in the chorus. He fell back onto the ground and got bit twice. He couldn't see where they were, he screamed as he crawled back to the door.

Teddy picked up a piece of two-by-four, outside of

the crawlspace, and held it like a bat ready to swing. The man emerged and stumbled to the ground. Teddy walked over to him.

"Couldn't find any liquor in there?"

"Snakes! Three of them got me. I heard the rattles and then they hit me."

Teddy helped him over to the tree and leaned him up against it.

"Where'd they get you?" Teddy asked.

"In my arm and my leg."

He lifted his hand up to show him.

"Keep your arm down. Below your heart. Let it bleed out so the venom comes with it."

"I have to get out of here."

"If those were rattlers, You aren't going to get too far," Teddy told him.

Teddy looked around and shook his head.

"I should just leave you here to die. Weber will probably reward me for getting rid of a thief."

"Please, please, you have to get help," the man begged.

"I'll try," he said.

Teddy walked over to Hildie's. He knew she wouldn't welcome him coming by at this hour, and neither would Mr. Weber. Though he figured Weber's anger might be offset by the fact that Teddy caught someone breaking into the Barn. He hesitantly knocked on the porch door. Footsteps approached. Hildie opened the door.

"Teddy, you can't come around here at this hour," she said.

"Hildie, I know. I wouldn't but I heard someone around the back of the Barn while leaving the restaurant. They broke into the crawlspace and ended up getting bit by a few rattlers. He's lying behind the building, probably dying. He begged me to go for help. I didn't know where else to go."

"Oh my God... Okay Teddy, you better go. I'll wake my father and he'll take care of it," she said.

She went inside and Teddy walked down the driveway. The light went on in the second-floor window.

15

It was the following evening when Teddy returned to the Silver Lake Inn. The man was gone when he walked up from behind the Barn. The crawlspace door had been repaired and there was no sign of the disturbance. He wondered if Weber had helped him or the man crawled away. For all he knew, Weber might have dragged him into the woods to die, although he probably just called Chief Lutz and had them haul him away to jail, if he survived the bites..

At the 2nd floor bar in the Barn, Teddy watched Al, the bartender, add water to bottles and write numbers on a scrap of paper. He held a bottle up to the light and swirled it around. The bartender's sleeve dropped and exposed boils on his arm.

When he finished filling bottles, he went to the

register, counted out money and shoved it in his pocket.

"A guy needs a living. Danke-Shane Weber."

Al walked behind Teddy and out the door. A moment later, Nelson walked in and sat next to Teddy at the bar.

"Well, we meet again. How goes it buddy?"

"Mr. Nelson, right?" Teddy asked.

"Just Nelson," he replied.

"Did you find your wife?"

"Nope. And that's one of the reasons this is still loaded," Nelson answered as he pulled the pistol from his jacket and placed it on the bar in front of him. "Boy, the service is sorely lacking up here, isn't it?" he asked as he stood and walked around behind the bar and poured a glass of whiskey.

"I don't understand. I thought you wanted to find your wife?"

"Oh, I do. I do. And then I'm going to kill her," he said as he downed his glass and poured another.

"Why?" Teddy asked.

"Why? Oh, boy. Listen Timmy..."

"It's Teddy."

"Teddy, I apologize. Anyway, you're young. You probably have your eye on some dame and dreams of a family like I did. I don't want to ruin that for you with my tales of marriage. You're going to have to find out the hard way... Let's have a toast."

Nelson walked over and poured Teddy a glass and raised his in the air.

"To unfulfilled dreams... Lies, really."

Teddy raised his glass, took a swig, and coughed. Nelson drained his, poured another, and walked back to sit next to Teddy.

16

The bowling ball hit to the right of the center pin and they all went down.

"Strike!" Bottles yelled.

He shuffled from the lane toward the seats and knocked the ash off his cigar. He picked up his glass to take a sip but realized it was empty, so he shuffled in his slippers and robe up the stairs to the bar and poured another from a pitcher.

Out the window he saw Lilian walking toward the house. He slammed his glass down on the bar.

"For fuck's sake. This crazy dame again. Why me, lord? Why me? How do I get rid of this broad? Where is that stiff Nelson to take care of her?," he asked himself.

He walked out the door to the patio.

. . .

TEDDY WALKED along the edge of the lake to the dirt drive. It was getting colder with winter setting in. Teddy thought it smelled like snow. It was quiet like before it snows, when the air is absent of any sound. He didn't hear any wildlife. No birds sung and he couldn't even hear the scurrying of a squirrel.

Past the trees, Bottles' house came into view. Then Lilian came into view, walking toward the house.

He stopped and watched her strut across the lawn up to the patio. Her overcoat was open and blew behind her, exposing her half-open white shirt. She looked angry and determined. He figured she had to be boiling with rage since the cold air seemed of no concern to her. She approached the steps and Bottles came out the door.

"Whoa, whoa. Lilian, what are doing here?"

"I'm here for you. You said we'd be together."

"Lil, we can't now. Not like this. It won't work. You have to move on."

"Move on? Move on? Really?"

Teddy crouched down in the brush.

"Lilian. Don't you see?"

"You're a genuine piece of work, Bottles Capone. You are."

"We're not the same anymore–You and me."

Teddy wondered what that meant as the spot on

his back suddenly struck him with an itch like he's never felt before and he grabbed a stick from the ground and used it to scratch. They both looked in his direction.

He ducked, and a car rolled up the road from behind him. He ducked down and watched the car drive onto Bottles' property. Bottles walked out to greet them. Lilian was gone. Teddy looked around but didn't see her anywhere. Bottles walked inside the house with his guests.

HE WALKED UP THE ROAD, remembering Bottles and Lilian's conversation. He thought about Hildie and wondered if they were the same or if they were too different to be together. She was from a wealthy family and he was a moonshiner's son. Could it ever work?

He wanted to see her again. He thought maybe he could catch her in her yard if he walked past, but he didn't want her father to see him. Mr. Weber was usually at the restaurant, so he figured the chance of him seeing him was slim. Especially if he was just walking down the road. He wouldn't go up to the house or anything, just see if she was out back in the yard.

He was treading a thin line. If they were to get

caught together, he could lose his job and not see Hildegard. He was sure Mr. Weber wouldn't approve of him. Maybe enough to hire him as a busboy, but not enough to be with his daughter.

17

Hildegard and Teddy walked out of the coatroom toward the front doors. He looked at her reflection in the large mirror as they past it. Her face radiated life, her hair tumbling across her cheek and over her shoulder, her light brown eyes. A twinge of a smile from the corner of her mouth. She glowed, and he felt a wave of warmth and love. He looked at himself, but he wasn't able to focus. He didn't recognize himself. The mirror was blurred, and he felt dizzy for a second, and grabbed onto Hildegard's waist as they exited through the glass doors and a cool gust of air blew across them. Hildie cinched her collar as the wind blew the bottom of her coat. They huddled together and hurried out toward the car.

"I can't believe you have a car, Teddy," she said.

"Me too, actually. Though it's not really mine, you know."

"That's okay, don't spoil it," she said.

They stopped short when they saw someone was sitting inside the car. The door opened and a man in a long black coat got out and approached them.

"Hello," Teddy said. "I... Bottles loaned me this car."

"Oh, yeah? Well, Bottles works for me. Sometimes he can forget that, and I have to give everyone a little reminder."

"If you need the car back, that's fine. You can take it."

"Oh, I don't need the car. I need more people to help me. Maybe since you're... shall we say between things? Maybe you want to sign up with me."

"Between things? You mean jobs? I have a job here. The Silver Lake Inn. I'm a busboy."

"Oh, really? You're a busboy. Here."

"Yes, for Mr. Weber..."

Teddy turned to Hildie and saw she was gone.

"Are you looking for someone?"

"My uh... Hildie. Hildie Weber. Her father owns this place."

"Oh yes. I know. I'm good friends with some of his patrons."

"I haven't seen you in there."

"I come from time to time. You know your girl-friend is from a wealthy family. This place is the only stop between Philadelphia and Atlantic City. And I don't know if you've noticed, but they make a good amount of money selling liquor, which some may frown on. Not me, of course. I'm all for it. But... her, coming from a wealthy family and all... you probably are a little worried you can please her. Being from a poor moonshiner family, yourself."

"How do you know..."

"Oh, it doesn't matter Teddy. But I know all about it. I only say this because I can help you. Make you a rich man. One that can please a girl from a rich family."

"What do I have to do?"

"Just signup with me."

"But I just got this job and..."

"You can keep you busboy job."

"I can? But what's the job then?" Teddy asked.

"You know Bottles and some of the clientele that patronize this place. Some of them are very rich and have everything they want. Bottles can get whatever he wants. You've seen that. But Bottles is a killer. A horrible person. Most of these people are the worst. Killers, liars, adulterers, thieves. And yet they have whatever they want... Don't you just a little want to get even? To get yours. Get what you want for a change?

Keep what you want... like that girl, Hildie. Make her happy."

"Sure, mister. But you haven't told me what the job is."

"Cinn, Manof Cinn," he said, extending his hand. "I know what it is like Teddy. When I was younger, my father kicked me out."

"How come?" Teddy asked.

"I was a little rebellious... But I had nothing. He even turned my best friends against me. They all turned. You have no friends Teddy. Remember that. You think you do, but you don't. They will all abandon you. But I won't. I can be your friend Teddy," he said.

"In my former life, status, they took everything I had from me. They left me to grovel in the dirt like a beast in the wilderness... And I swore I'd get even... And I've done alright. Now I'm offering you the same chance. Money, jewels, the love of a lady. You want that, don't you? More than anything? It almost doesn't even matter what the job is, does it? If it helps, you get what you want."

"I'm not gonna murder anyone, Mr. Cinn, if that's what you want."

"No, no, no. Nothing like that."

Mr. Cinn reached into his pocket and pulled out a gold eagle coin and handed it too, Teddy.

"Listen Teddy, I feel bad that I may have chased

your girlfriend away and ruined your evening. I want you to take her out and apologize for me. Show her a good time."

"I can't..."

"Take it. Take it. We can discuss how you can help me when we meet again."

18

They stood in line at the theater, waiting for the doors to open. A light snow fell, giving a magical sheen to the night. Money in his pocket, Teddy felt a foot taller and as though he was invincible for the first time in his life. He looked toward the street and saw an old war veteran in uniform sitting on the sidewalk, begging for change. In front of him was a small sign with words scribbled on it. He could read and write, but they weren't words he knew. It must be a foreign language, he thought. He almost walked over to the man when the theater doors opened. the crowd started moving, and he walked inside with Hildegard.

After the picture-show, Teddy pulled Hildegard by the hand toward the jewelry store as she resisted.

"Teddy, you don't have to buy me anything."

He stopped and stared at her as her eyes sparked with a light that warmed him.

"I want to Hildie, come on, it's fine."

"You shouldn't be spending that money. You don't know what he wants you to do for it."

"Nothing. He said this was just to make up for chasing you away the other night. Think what he'll pay when I work for him."

"That's not important, Teddy. There are things that matter more," she said.

"Stop being so serious, Hildie. Let me do this for you."

He pulled her onward and opened the door to the store. The bell rang over their heads alerting the man inside.

They browsed the cases and Hildegard looked past the fancy jewels and gold and gravitated to the cheaper religious medallions of the saints. She picked out a silver medallion with Saint Michael on one side and the Mother Mary on the reverse. He tried to get her to pick something more expensive, but she insisted it was what she wanted. He put it over her head and gave her a kiss.

They walked toward the door and heard a car crash outside of the store. A car had run into a tree in front of the store. A man lay on the hood of a car and blood ran down the window. Teddy raced to the driver-side of the car. The man's head faced him. He looked dead or unconscious. Teddy moved closer and the man's eyes briefly opened and he spoke.

"We're going to have fun, you and I," and he laughed.

Teddy looked at Hildegard as others rushed to the scene. He looked back at the man and his eyes were closed and any life seemed to have left his body. Teddy backed up slowly and walked to Hildegard.

"Is he dead?" she asked.

"Yeah, no. I don't know. I think so... He spoke to me."

"He did? What did he say?"

"He said we're going to have fun."

"What? Who?"

"I don't know. He and I? It was strange. He smiled and laughed after he said it."

"Come on, Teddy. I want to go home now."

————

TEDDY STOPPED in front of the driveway to Hildegard's house and watched her as she walked inside before driving away. He drove back to the center of town, where they saw the accident. The car was against the tree. The driver was gone.

He pulled over and examined the car again. He

looked inside the driver-side window and saw the dash-mounted compass. It moved. He wiped the glass to get a better view. The compass was spinning and not slowing down. He straightened up and turned when a man bumped into his shoulder. It swung Teddy around and left him, grabbing his shoulder. The man that bumped him stopped and faced him. He looked familiar. Teddy flashed back to the man's face lying on the hood of the car. It was him. The man smiled with a sinister grin and ran. Teddy yelled for him, but the man continued running around the corner. Teddy followed him into the alley behind the stores and lost sight of him.

He stopped to catch his breath and saw the sign in the window for "Madam Maria–Fortune Teller." A woman waved to him from inside the window. She motioned for him to come in. Teddy touched his pocket to feel the roll of bills buried there, looked around, and opened the door.

"Why are you here?" Maria asked as he sat down across from her at the table.

"You waved me in, remember?"

"Yes, but why are you here?"

"I want to know my future."

"No. I cannot tell you your future."

"I can pay."

"Only you can decide your future, now. There are

dark forces around you. They say you took something from them and now you are indebted."

"I have money. I can pay you."

"No. I will not take your money. It is false."

"It's as real as you and me."

"I'm afraid not," she said.

He stood and said, "You're crazy, lady," and turned for the door.

"You better get on your knees and pray. Like you never prayed before."

Teddy shook his head and walked out the door. He cursed her and walked toward the corner when a man appeared and sucker-punched him in the side of his head. Teddy collapsed and fell to the ground.

The snow turned to rain when he woke. He was soaked. He got to his feet and looked back at Maria's shop. The lights were now out and the sign in the window was gone. He moved closer and looked inside. The room looked empty, as though she moved out while he was unconscious. He reached into his pocket and realized they had robbed him. He Punched the window of Maria's door. The window cracked and he walked away.

He got to where he parked and saw the car was gone. So was the one that crashed into the tree. He walked through the rain toward home.

19

Teddy entered the cemetery and took a deep breath. He walked up the hill to his mother's grave. She was buried by his grandparents. They originally bought plots for the whole family. He got to his knees and took a deep breath. He missed her. She left when he was far too young.

He recalled her dressing him for his first day of school. She straightened his tie, and he ran to look in the mirror. He turned back to her, and she smiled as a tear ran down her cheek. He thought something was wrong and ran to her. She explained she was happy and proud of him.

She said, "If you knew how much I loved you, you would cry for joy, too."

They hugged, and he held her hand and walked him out the door and to school. He wished she were there with him, now. Only days after that first trip to school, he would be at that cemetery to see her coffin lowered into the ground.

He rose to his feet and turned to walk away when he noticed the fresh grave beside hers. It was his father's plot. He looked around, confused. There was no sign of who was buried there. He raced down the hill, out of the cemetery, toward his home.

Times were tough, and he figured his father must have sold the plot for cash. He vowed to himself that he'd make enough money and buy the plot back, even it meant paying to dig up whoever was there and move them. He couldn't keep his family together in life, but was determined they'd at least be together after death. At least their bodies, if nothing else.

He was walking down the White Horse Pike when he heard the horn honk behind him. He jumped out of the way of the car, pulling off the road. It stopped in front of him. Teddy paused, staring at it, and slowly approached the driver's side.

"I knew that was you! Where the hell you walking, boy?" Bottles asked.

"Mr. Capone..."

"Bottles to you, kid."

"I'm really sorry. Someone stole your car."

"What?" he asked.

"I took Hildie to the picture show, and when we got out of the theater, the car was gone."

"Hmm, maybe it was Jimmy. He could have seen it and took it back to the house. Don't worry. I'll find it. Get in. Let me give you a ride."

Teddy got in and they drove down the road.

"I don't think it was Jimmy. Someone knocked me out and took my money before the car went missing."

"Did you see who did it?"

"No, I was knocked-out. When I woke up, it was gone."

"You didn't see who clobbered ya?" Bottles asked.

"No, they sucker punched me from behind."

"With Hildegard there?"

"No. Well, it wasn't right when we got out of the theater. I took her home. There was an accident in front of the theater. This car smacked into the tree. The guy might be dead, I don't know. But anyway, Hildie wanted to go home after that, so I took her. But then I went back downtown, and that's when it happened."

"Geez. This story gets crazier by the second."

"'t's all true," Teddy assured him.

"Well, I tell ya Teddy, it's an evil world. You can't trust anyone these days... It's a good thing you're making friends that can look out for you. I hear you're going to be working for Manof."

"What? Mr. Cinn? No. How'd you hear that?"

"Word gets around. What do you mean, no?"

"I mean, I don't know."

"But he paid you already, didn't he?"

"What? No. I mean, he said it was for ruining my night because when he showed up, he scared Hildegard away."

"Oh, simple misunderstanding, I guess. No worry. I'm sure he'll make it right. You're making the right decision, kid. Everyone works for Mr. Cinn. Might as well just accept it now. Better to say yes now than find yourself there later. Know what I mean?" Bottles asked.

"Is it good money?"

"If it's money you need, he'll get you some. Money's nothing, kid. It falls like rain."

Teddy wondered what decision it was that he was making. Hearing Bottles say it was the right one made him question it. He saw him shoot Lilian. He even shot at him in the canoe! He thought back to that morning. Re-living it in his mind, he remembered something new. He got smacked on the back. It dawned on him it was the same spot on his back that kept bothering him. It must have been Dennis' oar that hit him. He recalled the events happening, but he heard Dennis splash in the water before he got knocked out of the boat.

"Hey, you daydreaming over there? Where do you want me to drop you off?" Bottle's asked.

Teddy had him drop him off at home. After getting out of the car, he turned back. Bottles winked and pointed at him with his hand as though he were firing a gun. Teddy walked toward his house.

20

Hildegard stood in front of the mirror as she finished putting on her black dress. She placed a silver cross necklace over her head and fixed it on her dress. She wiped a tear from her eye.

Mrs. Weber hollered upstairs, "Time to go."

Hildegard took a deep breath, went to her dresser, and blew out the candle burning in front of the Mother Mary picture. She looked in the mirror, fixed her hair, and went into the hallway.

"Father, we have to go, now," she said.

Mr. Weber asked, "What's the rush? He's not going anywhere."

"That's not funny, father," she said, and then muttered, "And I truly hope that's not the case."

"What's this?" her father asked.

"Nothing, talking to myself, again," she said.

"Better watch it, girl. If you start talking back I'm going to get worried."

The walked downstairs and out to the driveway. Mr. Weber drove to the cemetery and Hildegard sat in the backseat with her mother. Driving down the White Horse Pike, Hildegard saw Teddy walking along the side of the road, in the opposite direction. She jumped and turned to see if it was him.

"Hildegard, what is it? What did you see?"

"Oh, nothing. I thought I saw something. It must have been just a dog."

"Did you want to stop and talk to it?"

"No, Mother, I think we can let him be on his way."

"You always stopped to talk to animals since you were a little girl... Most people stop doing that when they get older, but you never did."

"No. I never did. I think it's a shame if most people do that."

"I'm not criticizing you, dear. I'm just saying that you are special, that's all."

"Well, thank you, mother, I think."

"I was talking to the snapper heads at the bottom of the barrel this morning," her father added.

"Not funny, father."

"They were talking back, too. You should have seen their little mouths moving, beep, beep, beep." he said, making an opening and closing movement with his fingers.

"Father," Hildie said.

"Really, father. We were having a serious conversation," Mrs. Weber said.

Mr. Weber pulled the car into the cemetery grounds.

21

Teddy was longing to see Hildegard again and tell her everything that had happened. He walked up her driveway and back steps and when she came out to meet him.

"Did you walk here, Teddy?" she asked.

"You won't believe what happened after I dropped you off the other night."

"I'm sure it'll be good. What happened?"

"They robbed me. They took my money and the car."

"Oh, my God," she said.

Together, they walked to Silver Lake while Teddy told her the details of what happened.

When they got to the lake, they were alone. He wanted to kiss her, so he was glad there was no one around. They sat on a bench together, looking out over the lake. He thought about the summer when he would watch Hildie swim. He couldn't believe they were together now.

He looked over at the hair blown across her neck and leaned in to kiss her. They made out and his hand reached her breast. Their tongues locked, and she moaned. He began unbuttoning her blouse and then she pushed back.

"We can't Teddy. It's cold, I'm freezing."

Teddy slid back, and she buttoned up her shirt and jacket. She stood and walked toward the bathhouse. He followed her behind the building, out of the wind and stopped her against the wall and tried to kiss her.

"Teddy, we have to talk," she said, stopping him.

"What is it, Hildie?"

"We can't keep doing this."

"Doing what?"

"This. All of it. I can't keep doing it. I don't think it's helping," she said.

"Helping who?" he asked.

"You," she said. "I tried to help, but you have to figure it out and move on."

"I don't want to move on. I want to be with you."

"It can't work between us, Teddy. I wish it could."

"Why? Because your family is rich and you father won't ever approve. I'm going to be rich, too, Hildie. You have to give me a chance."

"It's not that, Teddy. Not at all. There are things I can't explain."

"Sure."

"I mean it Teddy. It's not what you think. Nothing is!"

The itch was striking his back again, badly. It distracted him and he couldn't believe it was back clouding his mind, again. At this time.

"Hildie, don't do this. You're everything to me."

"I'm not. I can't be. I suppose you'll understand soon, but..."

He grabbed her arms and said, "Hildie, wait," but she escaped his grasp and just turned and walked back toward her house.

Teddy jumped backward and rubbed his back against the the corner of the building. He went to the thirty-foot slide and climbed the stairs to the top. Stars blanketed the sky and reflected across the water. He could see the Milky Way. The wind was blowing and his wiped the tears from his eyes. He pushed off and slid down the slide toward the lake. At the bottom he slowed himself with his hands and flipped over the side to the beach below.

He couldn't just let her walk out of his life. As he headed toward Ohio Ave that ran to the back of Hildie's, he saw the veteran beggar from a few nights before. He reached for his pocket and remembered he was broke again.

"I wish I could help you." Teddy said as he neared the man.

"I'm here to help you," the man answered.

"Unfortunately, I don't think you can, unless you're hiding a trunk of money somewhere."

"Money can't buy back your soul, Teddy," the man replied.

"Ha. Well, right now, I'm dead-broke with a rich girlfriend that left me. Good luck to you, but I have to get her," teddy said as he walked away and picked up his pace toward Hildie's back yard. Half-way there, he realized the man said his name. He stopped in the road and considered going back to ask him, but then continued on his way, thinking he may have misheard him.

22

He smelled smoke and heard voices as he followed the trail along the creek through the woods. Two boys sat around a campfire. Teddy said hello, but they ignored him and didn't turn to look. He walked along the trail out of the woods at Silver Lake.

Three kids launched a rowboat and an older couple holding hands sat on the bench. A man stood in the distance near the slide, with his back facing Teddy. As he got closer, the man turned, and he saw it was Mr. Cinn.

"Teddy, how fortunate to run into you."

"Hello, Mr. Cinn."

"Call me Manof," he said.

"Yes, sir."

"So polite. I like that."

"Listen, Teddy. Do you want to make some money?"

"Yeah, I do. I really need it, actually. They robbed me of what you gave me last time."

"Robbed? Really? That's awful. What's this world coming to?" he asked.

"I don't know."

"Well, anyway, it's an easy job, really. You know that still operation set up in the woods near Rowan's lake?"

"Yeah, you know about that?" Teddy asked.

"I know about all the moonshine operations, Teddy. Most of them are mine."

"I know some shiners. I don't want to do anything to hurt them," Teddy said.

"Oh, no. Don't worry. I just need you to create a brief distraction at midnight tonight. Something to get them away from the still. You should be able to handle that, no problem, right?"

"I guess."

"Here, take this," he said as he handed him a pistol. "maybe fire a few times to get their attention. You can figure out the details."

TEDDY WALKED along the dirt road when he saw the

two kids from the campfire fighting over a Three Musketeers candy bar.

"Give me it, it's mine," the first boy said as he reached for it.

"You said you'd share. Indian-giver. I want half," the second said as they wrestled.

"No, I'm not giving you any now."

Teddy kept walking.

———

SOME TIME NEAR MIDNIGHT, he quietly approach the area where the stills were set up. He heard voices, crept closer, and saw four men. His pocket watch read quarter to twelve. He had some time. He backed up and sat down against a tree. The stars twinkled in the trees. He thought back to sitting at his father's still at night. Then he thought again about the grave next to his mothers. He wanted to go back and see if there was a tombstone and a name yet. He looked at his watch, shoved it back in his pocket, grabbed the pistol and stood when...

An EXPLOSION rang out.

He saw a fireball through the trees. The still had blown. He heard men screaming and two gunshots. A man ran through the trees engulfed in flames.

Another man burst through the trees in front of

him, screaming. He ran straight at Teddy while pointing a pistol at him. Teddy raised his gun and fired two times. The man fell and hit the ground in front of him. Teddy stood staring at the burning body on the ground. The man had his hand outstretched. There was nothing in it. He turned around in a circle, looking desperately on the ground for the pistol.

More gunshots rang out, and Teddy ran through the woods. He ran until he had to stop to catch his breath. He leaned back against a tree and slid down to the ground. Recalling sitting at the still with his father and his partners, he wondered if he knew anyone that was at this still. He pulled off his hat and threw it into the trees.

He cried and wondered how everything got so complicated. Just days before, he was happily fishing in a canoe with Dennis. It seemed like a lifetime ago.

23

The light at the bar above the Barn was still on when Teddy entered. There was no one else at the bar. After a few drinks he put his head over his arms on the bar, and passed out. When he lifted his head, he was alone in the dark. He gulped down the drink in front of him and walked out.

He wandered the streets, stumbling in the middle of the road, until he found himself downtown in front of the theater and jewelry store where they saw the crash. He turned the corner and walked straight to Madame Maria's. The sign was in the window and the light was on. He opened the door and Maria was sitting in her chair.

"You! Get out. Get out. You can't be here."

"I can't be here? Why not?"

"Leave!" she yelled.

"I'm not going anywhere until you give me some answers, lady."

"I have nothing to give you."

"Were you a part of the robbery?" he asked.

"What are you talking about? I am no robber. Do I look like a robber to you?"

"Yes, you kind of do," he said.

"Get out!"

"When I left here the other night I was knocked out, my money and car were stolen."

"I know nothing about that," she assured him.

"Of course. What do you know?"

"I know you are in-between now," she said.

"In-between what?"

"You have to return to where it began."

"Where what began?" he asked.

"I see a lake. And a woman drowning. A boat with young men fishing, and demon that walks the earth. Go back to where you started. There you find answers. I can tell you nothing else. You must pray."

"Pray?" he asked. "Are you fortune tellers part of the church now? I thought you believed in magic and hocus-pocus stuff. Seeing the future in crystal balls and all."

"I show you the way, but you are blind. The answer is waiting for you at the lake. Be sure it is water and not a lake of fire you are entering. Go. Get out of here."

"Fine. I'm going," he said.

Teddy walked for the door as Maria pushed him from behind. He got outside and muttered, "Crazy witch... and religious, too."

He looked up and down the empty street and began walking toward Timber Lake. He walked through the trees to the lake as the sun rose.

A red police light flashed from atop the car, pulling up to the dam when he reached the shoreline. Two women stood by, watching. He followed the edge of the lake to see what was happening. They had found another body. It was a woman, in what looked like the same coat Lilian wore. He backed up, confused. *Was it her? When did it happen? Had she been dead all along? Who was the person he saw and talked to? Was she a ghost? Like he once thought. Or was she just recently killed?*

He tried asking a patrolman on the scene but the officer ignored him and kept about his business. Teddy sat on the hill looking out at the lake.

He wanted to tell Hildie, but was afraid she didn't want to see him. She'd probably think he was there to plead with her not to end their relationship and he knew he wouldn't be able to resist, too. *Everything had been going perfectly. How could it all go wrong?*

24

No one had reported the explosion. Everything was the same as before. Teddy found the two charred bodies and three others that looked like they had been executed. One still clutched a rifle in his hands and had obvious gunshot wounds to the chest. They shot the others in the head from close range. He recalled the man running toward him on fire. Except now he was no longer sure the man was pointing a pistol at him. He looked around the body and couldn't find it, if it did exist. Maybe the man was just running to him for help and he killed him. He sat taking in the scene when he saw an untouched jug on the ground. He opened it, smelled it, and took a big swig, coughed, and drank some more. Then he took the jug and began walking through the woods.

Teddy continued walking and drinking until he lost track of where he was. He emerged from the trees onto a dirt road. He looked both ways, took another swig and walked along the road. When the bottle was empty, he poured the last drops into his mouth and hurled it into the trees.

A car pulled over in front of him and sat idling. Teddy approached it and found Bottles behind the wheel.

"Teddy, where have you been? I've been looking for you. Manof wanted me to pay you for your troubles last night."

He handed Teddy an envelope with cash in it. Teddy took it and looked inside. Then stared at Bottles.

"Hey what's the problem?" Bottles asked. "Not enough. I'm surprised he's even paying you, since he said you didn't really do the job you were supposed to."

"What? What was that? I just went back and looked. They were all killed. No one said anything about killing anyone," Teddy said.

"You were supposed to distract them. You didn't do that. He said you went goofy and ran around executing them all, like a madman."

"No, I didn't. I shot one guy that was on fire running at me. I thought he had a gun."

"One guy? Instead of distracting them away, you

executed just one of them, but not the others? Are you sure? Looks like you had a bit to drink. Were you drinking then, too? Either way, you killed them all. If you had distracted them, they'd all be alive. Maybe you got a little carried away. Maybe it's a little fuzzy now. It's okay, I've been there. Trust me."

Teddy tried to remember the details of how it happened. Why didn't he fire the shots to distract them? Did he shoot others besides the one? Was he sure?

"I gotta go. You need a ride somewhere," Bottles asked.

"No, fuck you."

"Fuck me? Really? You got problems, kid. You better figure out who your friends are."

The car's tires spun in the gravel and drove away. Teddy threw the envelope at the car and the bills scattered across the road. He looked around and then began picking them up.

———

TEDDY WALKED along the main street when two scantly dressed women approached him. They struck up conversation and soon all three were walking together arm-in-arm to their apartment. Teddy caught the veteran out of the corner of his eye. He looked back and seeing it was him, shook loose the women's arms and walked toward him.

One of the women grabbed him and spun him back around and the other attached herself to his free arm.

"C'mon sweetie, it's getting cold out here. Would you rather be with an old bum or us cuddled under warm blankets?"

She put her hand on his crotch and gave a little squeeze.

"I think you'd rather be with us," she said.

They went to their room. Teddy could hardly look around as one was kissing him with her hand on the back of his head while the other undressed him. They sat him on the bed and undressed each other in front of him. One took off her shoe and threw it at the wall, hitting a small 8x10 framed picture. The only one hanging on the wall. They climbed into bed under the covers with Teddy.

WHEN HE WOKE to the sun was blinding him from the window. He rubbed his eyes and held his head, trying to recall what happened. He jumped up and found his pants and checked the pockets. There was a single dollar in the envelope. He looked out the window and saw no trace of them. The room was oddly empty of any personal items showing anyone was living there.

Teddy walked to the 8x10 framed print on the wall. He could barely make out the image through the grime and cracked glass. He wiped it with his hand and revealed the image of Mother Mary. He stared at it a moment, then walked to the door and scratched his back on the door frame.

25

He walked along the White Horse Pike, recalling what Madame Maria had said, "Pray, Pray." He stopped in front of St. Lawrence Church and stared for a moment before continuing to walk to the graveyard. He figured he could pray there, just as well. As he approached the gravesite of his mother, he saw that there were two open graves next to hers.

There was still no indication who they were for. Both remained unmarked. He knelt in front of his mother's tombstone, clasped his hands, and lowered his head.

He went to church school when he was little for a couple of years, but the 'Our Father' was the only prayer he could recall.

Our Father, Who art in heaven,

Hallowed be Thy Name.
Thy Kingdom come.
Thy Will be done,
on earth as it is in Heaven.
Give us this day our daily bread.
And forgive us our trespasses,
as we forgive those who trespass against
　　us.
And lead us not into temptation,
but deliver us from evil. Amen.

"Forgive me, Lord, for shooting that man. Though I don't think he could have survived, anyway. Maybe it was an act of mercy... Bless my mother and father, Lord. And if you could help me with Hildie, I could be so happy. Amen.

Leaving the graveyard, he saw Lilian walking in his direction with her head down. As he got closer to her, he tried to figure out what to say. She didn't look up or acknowledge him. He let her pass him, then turned and called her name. She stopped and slowly turned around.

"Lilian... I saw..."

"For Christ's sake, spit it out already," she said.

"Where are you going?" He asked her.

"I just heard the saddest story at the bar. They found a boy dead and when his father heard, he blew his head off with a shotgun. No one is left in the family to see them off. I was just going to pay my respects. No one should go like that."

She turned and began walking again when he stopped her.

"Lilian. I don't know how to say this, but I saw your body wash up at the lake."

"What are you talking about, kid?"

"The other day, I don't even know what day it was, but we were fishing in Timber Lake by Capone's house and I saw Bottles shoot you. You fell in the water and we got out of there and ran. He fired at us, too... But then the next day, I saw you alive. Or something."

"You're crazy, kid."

"I'm not, but I think you're a ghost. I just don't understand why I can see you."

Lilian started laughing. "Did Bottles put you up to this?"

"No. I'm serious."

"That's a good one, kid. But If I'm a ghost and you see me, maybe you're a ghost, too."

He watched her walk away toward the cemetery and called to her again.

"Lilian, what is the kid's name that died?"

"I only know that the mother died years ago and now they dug two fresh holes for the rest of her family. Poor woman."

He stared for a moment, thinking, and then ran down the road. He didn't get far before Manof's car pulled up alongside of him.

"Hey, Teddy. Looks like I'm your savior again. Where are you headed? Get in. I'll give you a lift."

Teddy stopped running, and the car came to a stop.

"Not you again."

"Whoa, now. Is that any way to speak to a friend?"

"Is that what we are now? Friends?" Teddy asked.

"Something like that. Get in, let's talk."

Teddy hesitated.

"You rather walk? It looks like you're in a hurry. I can get you there quicker than you can walk."

Teddy climbed in.

26

He ran up the steps and into his house. He saw his father standing by the fireplace lighting a pipe. It was a much younger version of him. He watched him walk in front of him to the other room where his mother knelt over the wash basin with him as a baby. His father leaned over and kissed his mother on the head.

Teddy slowly walked into the next room and looked around, but it was empty. He looked into every room. He got back to where he started and everyone was gone. Ha ran and pushed open the door. He leapt off the porch, over the steps, and ran up the road.

He got the back of Hildie's. Stopped and then ran to her back door and banged on it, calling her name. She opened the door and looked around.

"Hildie, thank God. You can see me?"

"Yes, Teddy. I can see you."

"I'm here, right? I'm here. I'm not... dead. You and me were together, right? That happened, the movies, the lake, we..."

She took his hand and lead him to the steps and sat down.

"It was all real, Teddy. I had a lot of fun but it can't last. I don't know how to explain it. They found your body yesterday."

"What? But..."

"I don't know why I can see you or how this is happening, but sometimes people get stuck here after life for a while before moving on."

"Why can you?"

"I don't know. I've always just been able to.., but never like this, Teddy. I know you. You're a beautiful soul, and you have to find God now and move on. Go to church and ask for forgiveness, pray."

"I don't want to go to church. I don't know church. I know you. I want to stay here with you."

"You can't. If not church, find him somewhere else. You have to or you could get dragged down into desolation."

Clouds moved in and the sky grew dark. The temperature dropped, and the wind picked up. Thunder rumbled and Manof's car pulled up at the end of the driveway. Manof got out and began walking toward them.

Hildie let go of Teddy's hand, stood, and began backing up.

"It's Manof Cinn," Teddy said.

"Teddy, stay away from him. Get to church, find God, find Jesus."

"I work for him."

"No," she yelled. "Do nothing for him. He is evil. He is the abomination. He will take you down to Hell."

Manof instantly got two-hundred yards up the driveway and appeared beside Teddy.

"Ready, Teddy? It's almost time."

Hildie ran inside the house and Teddy ran across the porch, jumped over the railing on the side, and toward the White Horse Pike.

THE GYPSY WAGONS where Dewey and Madame Maria lived were a half-mile down the road. Even though she chased him away, he thought she might be able to help him. Dewey ran from him, too, but at least they both could see him. He knew he needed help.

He ran up the dirt path through the trees to the wagons. No one was around. No one answered when he banged on their doors. He heard Manof's car getting closer. He ran across the street and into the woods.

He followed the path around Silver Lake and through the woods, past Bottoms Lake, toward downtown Clementon. He hoped he might find Maria at the shop he met her at before.

The sun was setting fast, and a stiff wind blew on the street.

27

Nelson was talking to Manof in the parking lot near the entrance of The Inn. He removed his hat and lowered his head. Manof gave him a friendly slap on the side of the cheek and handed him a set of keys.

Nelson grabbed the keys from him and got in the car.

"Wait," Manof said, and Nelson got out of the car and faced him.

Manof took out a pistol from inside his jacket and handed it to Nelson.

"Use this one. It will be more fun," he said.

Nelson got back into the car with the gun. The tires spun out in the gravel and he drove down the White Horse Pike. At New Freedom Road, he turned off to the right and went up the hill onto the dirt road around Timber Lake, toward Bottles' home.

He parked the car behind the tree-line where he could view the house. His hands clenched the wheel, lips pursed tight, and staring with a determined rage in his eyes.

He recalled the night he was home alone, drinking to squash down the pain of losing their child. His head was down and his eyes blurred from tears when he heard his wife enter behind him. She came in and threw her purse onto the couch. She stumbled a bit, and he knew she was out drinking again.

"Oh, for Christ's sake, Nelson. Grow up," she said. "You didn't have rods shoved up your twat. You know why? Because you don't have a pussy. You are the pussy. You're not a real man and if you were, you might have had your own kids. But they weren't yours, anyway. Because you're not a real man. Look at you crying like a little girl."

"What do you mean, they? You said they," he said.

"Oh just shut up. I'm going to bed. You can sleep on the couch. I can't look at you."

"What do you mean, they?" he asked again.

"Yes, they Nelson. They. There were two. Get over it because neither of them were yours. They were both his, Nelson. You weren't man enough to do it."

He recalled how his blood boiled and rushed to his head. He couldn't see straight and, without thinking, stood up and rushed behind her as she walked into the bedroom, punched her in the back of the head, and watched her fall on the bed.

"You piece of shit. Hitting a poor woman. You're no man. You're a sniveling little weasel," she said.

She then ripped her clothes off and lied on the bed with her legs spread.

"Look, you limp worm. Look. Get your last look because you'll never come near this body again."

HE TOOK the gun from his jacket, stared at it, got out of the car, and slammed the door shut. He stood staring and then reached into the car and blew the horn three times. Then waited.

Bottles walked out the door, and Nelson began his march toward him with the pistol in his hand.

"Jesus Christ. Why do I attract all the loons?" Bottles asked, rubbing his forehead. "Nelson, why do you want to come back here?"

Nelson extended his arm out in front of him with the gun pointed at Bottles.

"You ruined my life and now I'm going to take yours."

"You did that yourself, Nelson. Lilian was always a whore. I didn't make her that way. You're the fool that went ahead and married her."

"She was a dancer. We were in love."

"Oh, right? A dancer. You were in love."

"Go ahead, do it. What are you waiting for?" Bottles asked. "Fools and simps fall in love with whores, Nelson. Which are you?"

Nelson walked closer and fired three shots. Bottles look confused as the bullets entered his chest and stomach. The blood bubbled like boiling oil as he looked at the wounds. All of his skin bubbled and boiled. Bottles screamed and a burst of flame caught his clothes afire until his melting skin and blubber crackled in the flames. His bones showed and he let out a squeal and hiss as what it left of his twisted and scorched being ran off into the woods, like a wounded beast of the netherworld.

28

Teddy ran toward the alley where Madame Maria's shop was. The street was full of theater-goers and revelers stumbling from the speakeasy in the gristmill. As he got to the corner, he again saw the veteran holding his sign. His gaze fixated on it and he tried again to make sense of it.

"Quis ut Deus"

He looked up to see the man's face when he got bumped into by the woman he was with the other night.

"Teddy? Is that you?" she asked as she put her hand on his privates. He turned and faced her, then pushed her away and ran down the alley. At Maria's shop, he grabbed the door handle, but it was locked. He looked inside and saw her backing away. He punched the glass door and shattered it this time.

The roar of Manof's car engine came from the end of the alley. Its headlights shined on Teddy's face.

"Teddy, did you finally figure it out? What happened that day at the lake? There's nowhere for you to run. You're mine. You belong to me now. You took the job, you spent the money, you had your fun with the whores. Now you owe me."

"I don't owe you anything. I never agreed to anything."

"Yes, you did. You agreed when you took the whores. You agreed when you took the donuts, when you stole poor little Jeffrey's money, at the age of twelve. You have always agreed. You'd agree to anything to satisfy your greed for what you saw others had around you."

"No. No, I didn't."

Teddy fell to his knees and clasped his hands together tight as though he were crushing diamonds.

"Please God. Jesus, please forgive me. Deliver me from evil."

"He can't hear you now, Teddy. That time has long passed."

The veteran from the corner appeared beside Teddy.

"Leave him be. I have heard him." the veteran spoke with a voice that echoed down the alley.

His uniform changed from that of a soldier in the

war to one from a time long ago—something like a what gladiator wore. He wielded a sword that glowed with a fire.

"Michael," Manof said, recognizing the soldier.

"The Arch Angel?" Teddy asked.

The sky opened behind him and light shone forth.

Manof's clothes melted away and exposed a reddened body with a serrated tail and horns on his head. The creature let out a heinous squeal. It waved its arms and demons sprung from the walls of the buildings that lined the alley. There was thunder and lightning. The demons crawled across the walls and jumped from the rooftops. Their tortured screams filled the alley. Fire burst out everywhere and demons leapt at Teddy from all directions.

Michael yelled, "The Lord rebuke you," and he swung his sword and its flame swept through air and devoured all the demons within and without its reach. The sword's force snuffed out the Devil's fire and disintegrated the demons. The beast squealed and hissed as it flew through the alley into the darkness.

Michael reached out his hand, and Teddy took it.

THERE WAS a flash of light and a whiteout. Teddy was in back the canoe.

"You want to drown yourself, you stupid bitch?

Here, I'll help you," he shouted and pointed a pistol at her and fired three shots.

He watched Lilian splash into the water.

"Now it cost you everything," he said.

"Come on, let's get out of here," Dennis said, and they paddled toward the shore.

"Hey. Get over here, you little fucks." Bottles yelled.

They paddled faster. They were almost at the beach when...

"You hear me. Get over here, you little bastards."

Four more shots rang out.

One hit the trees on the shoreline, and one hit the water. Then one struck Teddy in the back. He fell into the water and the canoe tipped over.

29

Lilian walked out of the cemetery, along the White Horse Pike. Manof Cinn drove in the opposite direction, toward her. His car slowed to a crawl as he approached. It pulled alongside her, and she looked into Manof's eyes. He snarled, and the car sped away.

Lilian continued to the Church of Saint Michael on the edge of town. She entered the empty chapel and knelt at the altar and prayed aloud.

"Dear Lord, forgive me. I have not been good. I don't know how to do this. I am a wretched creature. I have committed many horrible acts. I have been unfaithful, and it has cost the lives of my dear husband and myself. I have ended the lives of my own children."

She thought back to the first time. Bottles threw a grand on the bed and said, "Take care of it." Take care of it. She didn't take care of anyone, she killed it. Like it was nothing. Sold her baby for some cash. For just the money needed to get rid of it. She recalled sitting on the bed, frozen in fear, crying. Bottles had done some bad things, but nothing was worse than what she did to her own children. She remembered she wanted to pray to God then, but she didn't know how. Could it be this simple? Just talking to God? Was he listening? Why should he take the time for a wretch like her?

The second one she considered keeping. Nelson was in tears when she lied to him and told him she had lost it. She didn't lose anything. She took the money from Bottles again to get rid of it.

"I deserve nothing and ask for only forgiveness with my punishments. I want nothing except to say I am sorry. Truly, deeply sorry. Please end this time here and send me where you must," she prayed.

The door to the chamber slammed open behind her and Nelson screamed, "LILIAN".

She turned and rose to her feet.

"Nelson, you followed me?"

"Yes, Lilian. And you came here to see Bottles, didn't you?"

"I did, Nelson, I did. I am so sorry, Nelson. I really am. For everything. You deserved so much better."

Nelson extended his arm straight ahead and pointed the pistol at her.

"Nelson, what are you doing?"

He fired three times. A cloud of smoke burst forth and when it cleared, Lilian was gone.

"Nooo," Nelson screamed as he pointed his pistol at the ceiling and fired until he was out of bullets. Plaster dropped from the ceiling around him and hit the floor. He put the gun in his jacket and walked out the door.

He got into the Silver Arrow and peeled out, leaving the parking lot.

30

He heard children playing. His mother's voice was calling him. He was a happy little boy. His mother and father were smiling as he ran to them in the yard. He saw himself swimming at the lake, the at his mother's funeral. Hildegard running into the water when they were younger, his whole life played out before him. And then everything melted away into a swirl of clouds, colors, and flashing light.

He heard a welcoming sound that enveloped him more than he heard it in his ear. His mother was there and hugged him while crying with joy. He saw his father smile with a happiness he'd never seen on his face before.

And Hildegard opened her arms to greet him.

"Hildie, but how?"

"Teddy, I knew you would make it."

"But are you..."

"Dead?" she asked.

"Yes, are you?" He repeated.

"No, not yet. I don't know how, it just is. I'm still in Clementon but here all time is now. The past, the future. Everything all at once. And it's beautiful. I have to go for a while, but I'll be back. There are others who want to see you."

He saw Lilian wave to him. Two small boys were with her.

Mother Mary appeared wearing a white scarf on her head, a brilliant blue robe over the warmest and inviting red dress. She extended her arms and embraced Teddy, smiling with tears in her eyes.

Behind her he saw his face.

31

Dennis walked out the restaurant's kitchen door, in between the restaurant and The Barn, and down the path toward the Weber home.

Hildegard was in the kitchen peeling eggs when she saw him pass from the window. She went to the door after drying her hands on her apron. Dennis walked up wearing his busboy white shirt and black bowtie.

"You're still in your uniform," she said.

"Yeah, I have to go back for another shift. I'm just taking a break to say hi."

They sat down on the porch steps.

"How are you doing?" Hildegard asked.

"I'm ok. I'm still just trying to get over what happened to Teddy... I wish you could have known him better. He'd be so jealous of me being with you.

Teddy really was smitten with you, though he never got the nerve to tell you... I still can't believe what happened."

"You really should tell the police what you know," Hildegard said.

"They're all crooks and grifters—friends with that hood. I see them drink together at the bar. They'll never nail him. I'll get rubbed out and end up floating in that lake."

"Maybe you should go back there. Maybe there's something you missed."

"I've been thinking about that," he said. He scratched his head and remembered something. "I have to go back to the restaurant, Hildie. I forgot to do something."

"Okay," she said. "I'll walk you back. I left something in the coatroom last night."

They walked together up the walk to the kitchen entrance. Dennis went down to the basement. Hildegard walked through the dining room. "Hello, Hildie," Giovanni said to her as she passed the buffet.

"Hello, Giovanni," she said, walking to the lobby.

She took a purse from a drawer in the coatroom. Then jumped backward, startled when she lifted her head.

"Goodness. Hello, Mary," she said. "You scared me."

Mary was the first ghost Hildegard ever encountered. She was just five or six when she met her upstairs in The Inn. She used to play with her dolls in the second-floor rooms when Mary would visit her and talk to her. They had many tea parties together. Her mother and father thought she had an imaginary friend, but Hildegard knew Mary was more than that.

She didn't understand at first why her mother and father couldn't see or hear her. She learned to stop mentioning her when she got a little older and her mother started talking about getting her some kind of help. It was around then that she started seeing others, too. There was no shortage of them around. Most were only around for a short time before moving on, but others were determined to stay.

"You did well, dear," Mary said.

"Mary, tell me why you haven't left?"

"The time's coming when I'll tell you what happened here."

32

It was late in the evening. The car sat idling with its lights off in the parking lot of The Inn. Nelson's hands clenched the steering wheel. The front door swung open and Bottles exited , fixed his coat, and walked down the stairs. Nelson revved the engine and turned on the headlights. Bottles stopped walking and faced the vehicle.

"Son of a bitch," Bottles mumbled and lit a cigar.

Nelson floored the pedal, the wheels spun, and the car raced toward him.

Thank you for reading *Dead at Silver Lake*!

I hope you enjoyed it. Please leave a review to help others find it, and check out the following pages for other fun stories.

Best Wishes,

TOM

WITCH HUNT 1730

A witch trial looms in the New Jersey Pine Barrens.

USA Today Bestselling Author Tom Schneider delivers a riveting historical thriller, staged deep in the pines of Mount Holly.

"A fun trip back in time that mixes horror and a crime story with Lenape Indians, witches, demons, and Ben Franklin."

HEADLESS 1776

The Headless Horseman Origin Story.

America wasn't the only thing birthed in 1776. The year also gave rise to the brutal terror of the Headless Hessian.

On October 24th, 1776 to Elijah sets off from Philadelphia on a trip to the village of North Tarrytown. There, his deeds give birth to a legend and his path leads to a showdown with the murderous horseman on All Hallows Eve.

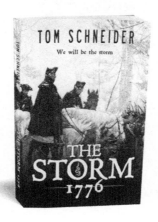

The Storm 1776

Christmas night, 1776. General Washington is losing the Revolutionary War. In a desperate attempt to turn the corner, he plans to cross the Delaware River and lead a surprise attack on Hessian forces in Trenton, New Jersey in the midst of a winter storm. Amongst Washington's troops is 14-year-old Nathan Smith, whose mother has just been murdered by a group of Hessian soldiers. While trying to care for his younger sister and track down his father, Nathan's manhood will be tested and transformed during his special war mission. In this epic tale of battle, tragedy, and independence, Nathan and his fellow Americans fight for freedom despite all the odds being stacked against them.

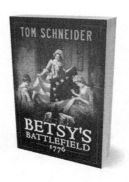

Betsy's Battlefield 1776

The untold story of how Betsy Ross helped Washington save the American Revolution.

During five days over Christmas in 1776 Betsy Ross delays Colonel Von Donop and 2,000 Hessian forces in Mount Holly, 20 miles south of Trenton, while Washington executed a surprise post-Christmas attack.

In the first successful American undercover operation performed by a woman, with the fate of the nation in the balance, Betsy engages the colonel and prevents him from thwarting Washington's offensive.

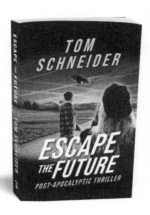

Escape The Future

After the power grid goes down and the death of their parents; Henry, Eva, and Layla are left alone in a dark, desolate and dangerous world, with only their father's dying words - stay together.

When Eva gets nabbed in a roundup, she confronts greater threats than she ever imagined, while Henry and Layla search for her, facing their own imminent peril.

 Up against the mysterious forces of a conspiracy that may go beyond this world, they fight to stay together, stay alive and escape the future.

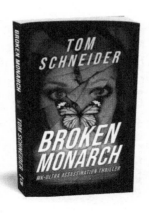

Broken Monarch

MK-Ultra Assassination Thriller

In 1979, Glenn is a chef at the Silver Lake Inn when his experiences of lost time become inhabited by a violent and dangerous part of himself he doesn't know.

A week before the First Lady of the United States' visit to the restaurant, he meets Lindsey, who holds the key to understanding what's happening.

The clock is ticking as he uncovers the mystery of their shared past, his part in Project Monarch, and the plot to kill the First Lady.

Can they figure it out in time to escape the program, save the First Lady, and save themselves?

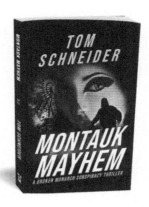

Montauk Mayhem.

In 1983, Glenn is on the run from the Monarch Project when Robin's son goes missing from a Montauk carnival. Glenn's search to find the boy uncovers a conspiracy beyond kidnapping right back to the program he is trying to escape.

A sexy fortuneteller holds the key. But can he unlock the puzzle in time to find the boy while battling old demons and new monsters?

Glenn must choose to save himself from the program or try to rescue Robin's son from a future of hell.

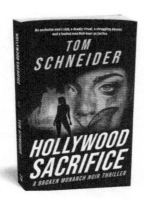

Hollywood Sacrifice

An exclusive men's club, a deadly ritual, a struggling dancer, and a hunted man hell-bent on justice.

In 1984 when Monarch Project assassins track and hunt Glenn, he meets a stripper that could help him turn the tables and be the hunter, but first, he may need to help her. As a struggling dancer at the Hollywood Showcase, Casey's desperation to raise money for her sister's surgery leads her into the arms of the same threat facing Glenn.

Together they discover the evil they face is more horrific than imagined. Can either of them survive? Will they save each other?

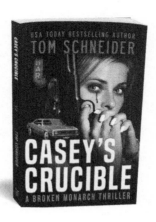

Casey's Crucible

In a time of murder and deceit, love can be a trap.

In 1985, Glenn, a forlorn, on-the-run former government assassin, re-enters the United States to find Casey, his ex-lover. But Casey is about to discover her modeling agency recruit dead in her boss's mansion, and find a dark side of his background that threatens her and Glenn.

Eluding hired assassins, the FBI, and Casey's well-connected boss, Glenn tries to reunite with Casey but she may be his biggest threat as she confronts love, desperation, and her own past.

Made in the USA
Monee, IL
27 December 2022